Library of Congress Cataloging-in-Publication Data
LaReau, Kara.
Rocko and Spanky have company/written by Kara LaReau; illustrated by Jenna LaReau.
p. cm.
Summary: Rocko and Spanky, twin sock monkeys, get ready for a visit from their mother.
[1. Monkeys—Fiction. 2. Toys—Fiction. 3. Twins—Fiction. 4. Mother and child—Fiction.]
I. LaReau, Jenna. Ill. II. Title.
PZ7.L32078Rr   2006
[E]—dc22   2004005738
ISBN-13: 978-0-15-216618-2
ISBN-10: 0-15-216618-1

First edition
A C E G H F D B

Printed in Singapore

Color separations by Bright Arts Ltd., Hong Kong
Printed and bound by Tien Wah Press, Singapore
This book was printed on 104 gsm Cougar Opaque Natural Woodfree Paper.
Production supervision by Ginger Boyer
Designed by Jenna LaReau

ROCKO and SPANKY HAVE COMPANY

Written by **Kara LaReau**

Illustrated by **Jenna LaReau**

Orlando   Austin   New York   San Diego   Toronto   London

Rocko and Spanky are twins.

"We're having company today," says Spanky.

"Hmm," says Spanky. "Maybe we should tidy up."

"Yeah. PRONTO," says Rocko.

"I'll put away the clothes," says Rocko.

"And I'll put away the toys," says Spanky.

"Now I'm cleaning the kitchen," says Spanky.

"And I'm sweeping the floor," says Rocko.

"I'll take out the trash," says Spanky.

"Then I guess *I'll* be cleaning the stairs," says Rocko.

"All that cleaning made me tired," says Rocko.

"Urp! Me, too," says Spanky.

"Now, what should we serve our guest?" asks Spanky.

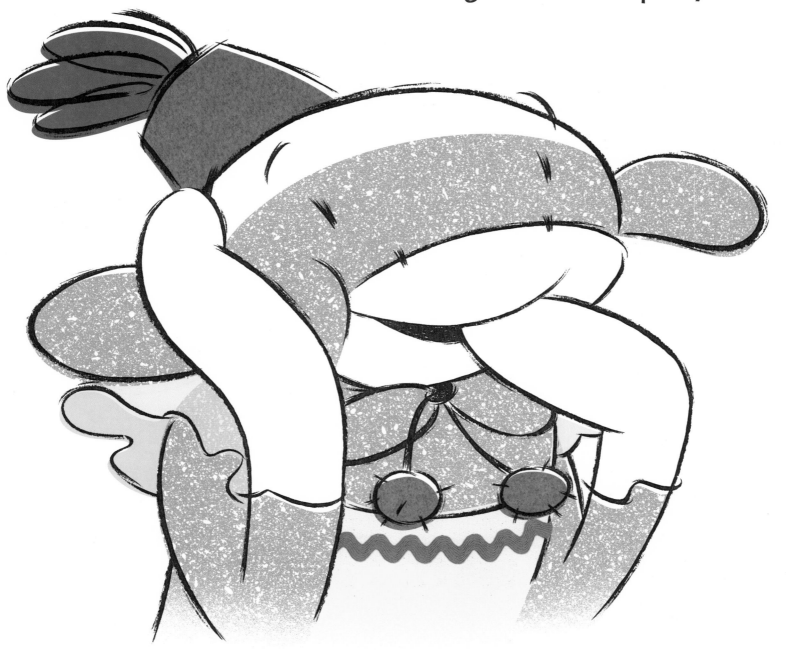

"I know—peanut-butter-and-banana sandwiches!"

"Sounds good," says Rocko.
"Except we're out of bread. And peanut butter."

"And bananas," says Spanky.

"I'll go to the store," says Rocko.

Rocko does the shopping.

"I'M HOME!" calls Rocko.

"Our guest will be here any minute," says Spanky.
"Did you get everything we need?"

"I got Coco-nut Soda and marshmallows," says Rocko.
"And Rain-bo Sugar Loops—with a FREE Super Ball inside!"

"No bread? No peanut butter?
No *bananas*?" asks Spanky.

"Um . . . ," says Rocko, "wanna play with my Super Ball?"

"Oh no!" says Spanky. "Our company is here."

"MOMMA!" say Rocko and Spanky.

"Hello, my little monkeys," says Momma Socko. "I've missed you!"
"We've missed *you*," says Rocko.

"I brought goodies," says Momma Socko.

"And I made your favorite—

peanut-butter-and-banana sandwiches."

"You're the best," says Spanky.
"Wanna play with my new Super Ball?" asks Rocko.

"Of course," says Momma Socko.
"How about a game of monkey in the middle?"

"I'll just hang up my sweater."

"Uh-oh," says Spanky.

"Nice job putting away the toys," says Rocko.

"Um . . . ," says Spanky, "anybody want a sandwich?"

Rocko may not like the way Spanky cleans,
and Spanky may not like the way Rocko shops,
but they still love each other.

And they LOOOOOVE company.

"I'm having a *ball*," says Momma.
"Not if we can help it!" say Rocko and Spanky.

Treat Your Guests to
MOMMA SOCKO'S
Deee-licious
Peanut-Butter-and-Banana Sandwiches
(serves 4)

Ingredients:

8 slices of bread (Momma's favorite is cinnamon swirl.)

Peanut butter

2 large bananas, sliced into circles

For extra pizzazz, add coconut flakes, chocolate chips, raisins, mini marshmallows,

or any other tasty treats your guests might like.

Step 1) Spread lots of peanut butter on one side of each slice of bread.

Step 2) Divide banana slices so you have enough for each sandwich. Lay bananas on 4 slices of bread.

ep 3) Sprinkle with pizzazz.

Step 4) Top with remaining slices of bread. Squish each sandwich so ingredients really stick together.

ep 5) Ask an adult to help you toast the sandwiches in a toaster oven (or fry them in a pan), if desired.

ep 6) If you like, cut sandwiches in halves or fourths. (Don't cut the crusts off — they're good for you!) For an extra-fancy look, insert cocktail toothpicks skewered with mini marshmallows.

ep 7) Serve to your guests. And, of course, save some for yourself!

ON'T FORGET: The only thing better than having a DEEE-licious treat is sharing it with company!